WHADDAYAMEAN

For my mother and father, who
would have liked to change the world

Published by Crown Publishers, Inc., a Random House company,
201 East 50th Street, New York, New York 10022.
Published in Great Britain in 1999 by Jonathan Cape Ltd.

CROWN is a trademark of Crown Publishers, Inc.

www.randomhouse.com/kids

Printed in Singapore

Library of Congress Cataloging-in-Publication Data
Burningham, John
Whaddayamean / John Burningham. — 1st American ed.
p. cm.
Summary: When God sees what a mess has been made of the world,
God gets two children to convince everyone to help make it the lovely place it was meant to be.
[1. God—Fiction. 2. Environmental protection—Fiction.]
I.Title.
PZ7.B936We   1999
[E]—dc21   98-44159

ISBN   0-517-80066-7 (trade)
0-517-80067-5 (lib. bdg.)

10 9 8 7 6 5 4 3 2 1

First American Edition

WHADDAYAMEAN

JOHN BURNINGHAM

CROWN PUBLISHERS, INC. 👑 NEW YORK

It took millions of years to make planet Earth, and God was very pleased when finally there was a paradise where animals and people could live, with air to breathe and water to drink.

God was tired after making planet Earth and went to sleep for a very long time. Then one day, God woke and decided to visit the planet that was paradise. But not wanting to be seen, God caused a deep sleep to fall upon the people.

And while everybody slept, God started to look around the world. There were two children who were playing under a very large and old cedar tree who had not gone to sleep. And God came to them and said, "Why are you not asleep like everyone else?"

"We are not asleep," said the children, "because we are playing a game under the cedar tree."

And God said, "Since you are not asleep, you must come with me and look at my world."

And so the children set off with God to look at the world.
And God said, "I do not like the things I see."

"The waters of the sea, which I made for the fishes and the birds, are filthy and dirty."

"The air, which I made clean and fresh for you to breathe, has been filled with fumes that are foul and nasty."

"The forests, which are home to the plants, birds, and animals, are being chopped down and burned. Many living things have gone forever and I cannot make them again.

"There seem to be an awful lot of you people. I made you the most clever of all creatures so you would look after the world."

"And look at the ice, which I made for the penguins
and polar bears. It is melting now and getting very thin,
and parts of the world will soon be flooded."

"There are many of you who do not have enough to eat, and there are many who seem to have too much. You have spoiled my lovely world."

"We're only little children. We're not old enough to spoil your world. What do you want us to do?"

They had stopped in a place that God liked, and they had a picnic. And the animals and birds came too, for they had no fear because God was there. And God said, "You must go and tell the grownups to change the way they are living."

"Grownups won't listen to us," said the little children.

"They will listen if you tell them that I told you to," God said. "I will come back again when the world is a better place."

And so the little children set out to find the men with the money who cut down the trees, dirtied the waters, and fouled the air.

"We must save the world," the children told them. "Stop cutting the trees, dirtying the waters, and fouling the air."

"Whaddayamean? Don't waste our time, you snotty little kids. You can't tell us what not to do. Run away, we're busy."

"But God said to tell you not to cut down the trees, dirty the waters, and foul the air."

"Oh, if it was *God* who said we must not do this, then we must stop," said the men with the money.

The children went to see the people who said they spoke
for God and who were always quarreling amongst themselves.

"We must save the world. You must stop quarreling
amongst yourselves."

"Whaddayamean, you foolish little children that have lost
your way? You cannot tell us not to quarrel amongst ourselves."

"But God said to tell you," answered the children.

"Oh, if *God* said to tell us, then we must all stop
quarreling," said the people who did speak for God.

Seawolf submarine nuclear-powered to complement the current fleet of attack submarines. Intercontinental Stealth Bomber, designed for "time-critical" targets, nuclear and conventional. Aegis guided missile destroyer, intended for defense of air craft carriers. Joint Stars, a 707-class

Joint Stars, a 707-class aircraft operate a target-attack radar system. **$387,000,000**
Hornet twin-engine strike fighter for defense. **$50,000,000**

Trident II, submarine-launched ballistic with ten nuclear warheads. **$50,000,000**

Multiple launcher rocket system load ballistic rockets; a long-range self-p artillery weapon widely used in the Gulf **$29,000,000**
Abrams M1 tank, upgraded with improve and nuclear/biological/chemical protection **$5,800,000**
Tomahawk cruise missile for conventi nuclear-armed, surface ship or submarine

Ground-launched tactical missile system deep fire in nearly all weather conditions. **$1,100,000**
Intercontinental Stealth Bomber, "time-critical" targets, nuclear and **$2,200,000,000**
Laser-guided air-to-surface missile, pi surgical-strike capability for attack helico operate a target-attack radar system. **$59,000**
Hornet twin-engine strike fighter for defense. **$50,000,000**

Trident II, subma -launched ballist with ten nuclear w eads. $969,000,000

Multiple launcher cket system loa ballistic rockets; long-range self- artillery weapon w y used in the Gul

Abrams M1 tank, aded with impro and nuclear/biologi chemical protecti

Tomahawk cruise ssile for convent nuclear-armed, surf ship or submarin

Ground-launched ta al missile system deep fire in nearly weather conditions

Wide-area smart m soldier portable, targets within 100 r ers.

Abrams M1 tank, upgraded with i nd nuclear/biological/chemical protec

Trident II, submarine-launched ballistic

e launcher rocket system loade stic rockets; a long-range self-r artillery weapon widely used in the Gul

Then the children went forth to see the men who had the guns and the bombs that hurt and that killed.

And the children said, "We must save the world. You must throw away those horrid things that hurt and kill."

"Whaddayamean, you silly children? You can't tell us what to do with our guns and bombs."

"We *can* tell you," said the children, "because God said to tell you."

"Oh, if *God* said so, then we must throw away the guns and bombs," said the men in the uniforms.

Finally, the children gathered together all the people who stood by and took no notice of what was happening to the world.

"We must save the world. Look at what is happening. You must change your ways."

"Whaddayamean, you horrid little whining brats?" shouted the people. "Who do you think you are, telling us what to do?"

"But it is *God* who said to tell you to change your ways to save the world."

"Oh, if it is *God* who said we must change our ways, then we must change at once," said the people who took no notice of what was happening around them.

And so it came to pass that the men with the money stopped cutting the trees, dirtying the waters, and fouling the air.

And those who said they spoke for God stopped quarreling amongst themselves.

And the men in the uniforms who had the guns and the bombs that hurt and killed people threw them away.

And the people who stood by and took no notice of
what was happening to the world changed their ways.

And those who did not have enough to eat had
enough to eat.
And the world became a better world.

And time did pass. And God decided to visit the world and returned to the cedar tree where the children had been playing. And God called to them and said, "Show me my world."

The children went to their mother and said, "Can we show God the world?"

And their mother said, "Go and show God the world, for it is a lovely world. But don't be late for bed. Remember, you have school tomorrow."